I'm Invisible

I'm Invisible

ALDIVAN TORRES

Canary Of Joy

CONTENTS

1   1

I'm Invisible
Aldivan Torres
I'm Invisible

Author: Aldivan Torres
© 2020- Aldivan Torres
All rights reserved.

This book, including all its parts, is protected by Copyright and cannot be reproduced without author's permission, or transferred.

Aldivan Torres, born in Brazil, is a consolidated writer in various genres. So far, the titles have been published in dozens of languages. Since his age, he's always been a lover of the art of writing, having consolidated a professional career from the second semester of 2013. Your mission is to conquer the heart of each of your readers. In addition to literature, its main amusements are music, travels, friends, family, and the pleasure of life itself. "For literature, equality, fraternity, justice, dignity, and honor of human being always" is your motto.

Book Content
I am invisible 1
I'm invisible 2
I AM INVISIBLE 3
I am invisible 4
I am invisible 5
Trip to an island- I'm invisible 6

I am invisible 7

I am invisible 1

Family room
Dad
My God, what is this?
Trans
I am your daughter, father. I finally wanted to take this on board. Furthermore, I was feeling suffocated trying to make a character to please you. But I wasn't being happy that way. I have the right to express myself as I am and as, I think.
Dad
You have no right to anything. You are a freak. This is your fault, woman. Look what gave your good treatment to this boy? He became a sissy.
Woman
It wasn't my fault, love. This one came with a factory fault. I suspected. And now? What will we do? How we're going to tackle society? This is a shame!
Shemale
I am not a shame. I am a human being with values. Furthermore, I am your daughter. Moreover, I need your support.
Dad
You are no longer my son! I had a son, but now he died. As of now, it no longer exists.
Mother
We need to act quickly before the neighbors know. Go pack your things to go away. Anyone who asks, we'll fashion a story. But you will not take away our family's honor. You have no right to destroy us. We have no responsibility for your problem. You are already of legal age and have your job. Then go away!
David

But mom, weren't you the one who recently rocked me on your lap and said you loved me? What happened?

Mother

I swear, if I knew, an abortion was better. Better an abortion than a transsexual!

Dad

Calm down, woman! Do not exaggerate! Let him go! Boy, do not regret your decision because you will never have our family by your side again. This is definitive!

David

I am disappointed. You have never understood me or supported me. But I did not expect such a strong reaction. You never loved me! You are hypocrites! Furthermore, you prefer to please society than having a daughter by your side. I want to see if society will support them in old age. You will be thrown into the asylum and will suffer a lot. Nobody will take care of you. I am your only daughter. But you despised me because of prejudice. Let it be! The future will show who is right. I swear to myself that your abandonment will not destroy me. I want to marry and have my kids. Because I deserve to be happy!

Mother

David, don't talk nonsense. You just entered a world of pain without consulting us. You put our reputation at risk. What did you expect? Flowers? Do not be silly. The world is made up of appearances.

Dad

I don't know if you know. But Brazil is the country that kills most transvestites and transsexuals in the world. Your destiny is death.

David

I don't believe you. I have a God who will always protect me. "Even though I walk through the darkest valley, I will fear no evil, for you, are with me; your rod and your staff, they comfort me".

Mother

Who is this God, you fool? A God who allows children to die in an accident? Don't be silly.

Dad
The evil on earth is very great. Nobody can save you.
David
Stop it! I will survive! I won't listen to it! Furthermore, I'm leaving to live my life. Goodbye!
Looking for an apartment
David
Good morning, I'm looking for an apartment for rent.
Man
I rent. What are you looking for?
David
A simple apartment. Small, comfortable and cheap.
Man
All right. I have one in that style. But you have to follow the rules of the condominium: no parties, pay the bills on time and respect everyone. That's going to be difficult. You know that transsexuals are not respected by anyone.
David
I know that. I promise that I will follow all the rules.
Man
It's ok. Be welcome.
David
Thank you so much for this!
At work
David
Good morning, boss. I arrived with my new look. I'm really excited to work.
Boss
David, what a surprise! I didn't know you were a transsexual.
David
Yeah. Does that change anything?
Boss

Unfortunately, everything changes. My company has always valued morality. I don't want your name associated with my company. You are fired.

David

I swear I don't understand. Last week, you confided in me that I was your best employee. Doesn't that count in my favor?

Boss

Excuse me. Don't take it personally. This is a strategic decision. I want to avoid conflicting with customers because of you. I need to preserve the company at all costs. You have the skills to try to get another job. I wish you the best of luck with it.

David

Okay, then! I have no hard feelings. It will not destroy me. Thank you for believing in my potential. It was excellent for a while.

Boss

Glad you finally realized it's the best way forward. Good luck.

David

Thank you very much, boss.

I'm invisible 2

Psychological session

Psychologist

Good morning, David. I'm so glad you came. What is the reason behind this?

David's transsexual

Good morning, doctor. Since I became a transsexual, bad things have happened to me: My parents kicked me out of the house and I lost my job. I'm still shaken up. So, I'm here.

Psychologist

That's from today's good times, apparently. However, as it is something new, many people reject and persecute transsexuals. There are many cases of violence against this group. I really admire your courage.

David

I am also proud. Furthermore, I know I made the right decision despite the setbacks. I got rid of a character, and I'm being myself. This greatly improved my self-esteem. However, this is not going to be easy. I understand that I am the human scum in the opinion of the majority. It will be a great challenge to live in society with monsters, as if they were masters of the truth. But I need to face the situation. I have no other choice.

Psychologist

You are free to choose your path. Just be good and sure you don't cross them. Don't put yourself in any danger. These people are conservative, prejudiced snobs.

David

I know that. I will take care of myself in the best possible way. We live in a hypocritical world. During the day, men come to me and at night they judge me as if I were an animal. The important thing is to maintain appearances of false morality.

Psychologist

Most of those who persecute their community are people who're in the closet. That is why they are angry with those who assume their sexual identity. There is a conflict of ideas and interests. They are individuals who need psychological treatment.

David

I understood. What are my worst enemies now?

Psychologist

Religious fanatics. They are despicable and prejudiced beings. Be cautious with them. Above all, seek your safety. Do not trust anyone.

David

I got it. I want advice. Furthermore, I want my life back.

Psychologist

Getting a formal job will be very complicated. So be a freelance salesperson in the area in which you will be working. Regarding love, be discreet. Seek long-lasting relationships with trusted people. Don't be a prostitute.

David

Good advices. I also want to study. What do you recommend?

Psychologist

Sexology. It is a specific course with a healthy understanding of sexuality. This will give you important answers about yourself.

David

I loved the tip. I got to go. Thank you very much, Doctor.

Psychologist

No need to thank. I just did my duty. Good luck with your projects.

At the bar with gay friend

Friend

How was the doctor's appointment?

David

It was a fruitful experience. We talked openly about several subjects. This made me reflect a lot.

Friend

Great. You need this. I know it's not easy to overcome what you went through. Go back there as many times as you wish.

David

That is what I will do. And you? You have already taken up your sexual identity for your family?

Friend

God forbid. I am not strong like you. For my parents, I will always be their pride. I even have a girlfriend, so they don't get suspicious. But actually, I like men. I have discreet relationships with men. But it can never be revealed. I need to be well regarded by society.

David

I understand your position. You are not the only one to think that way. Many men think the same. You have to keep appearances and be happy. I am just an exception.

Friend

That's why we admire you. We will support you. Have you thought about what work you will develop?

David

I'm going to be a street vendor. I'll sell ice cream. Furthermore, I will work all day on the streets. In the evening, I do a course. I chose sexology.

Friend

Wonderful. You have a lot of disposition. I know you suffered a lot from the rejections, but I don't think it will bring you down. You are very talented and hardworking.

David

I have no other choice. I will fight for what I believe. Furthermore, I hope you support me. I'm going to need many positive vibes.

Friend

if it depends on me, you are already victorious. I'm at your disposal. I am your true friend.

David

Thank you so much for this. You must know how important it is to have true friends.

Friend

You are completely right. Much peace, health, success, and victories for you.

David

So be it. God bless us.

I AM INVISIBLE 3

AT SCHOOL

classmate

I'm going to leave! Furthermore, I want to avoid sharing the same space with an aberration.

Divine

You can leave! We're fine without you!

David trans

Very well! The humiliated will be exalted. We deserve respect!

Divine

Exactly. Let's take a break to talk?

David trans

It will be an honor to get a meeting with a person as cool as you. I guess that's the irony of destiny!

Divine

It's really incredible. Start with yourself. Could you tell us a little about yourself?

David

It's all right. My name is David and I'm a transsexual. It was not long ago that I assumed my sexual orientation. After my decision, everything in my life changed. I was kicked out of the house and lost my job. It was a very difficult situation that I still haven't got over.

Divine

I imagine how difficult it must have been for you to make this decision. I support your cause. Furthermore, I am the protector of minorities and the poor. Truly, I tell you: I would like a fair and liturgical world, but that is not the reality. Evil and prejudice will always exist in humanity. It is up to us to fight against it and promote the good.

David

Your words touch me so deeply. Who are you? A Prophet?

Divine

I am "The son of God". I came from space to try to set an example for humanity. Day after day, I am evolving and doing good. This is more than a mission. It is a must for me.

David

Those are gorgeous and very moving words. But what is your opinion of me? Do you want to reject me?

Divine

I love you just the same. In fact, even more than the others. Since I met you, I sympathized immediately. I already consider you a friend.

David

Unbelievable! You're the first person who accepts me as I am. You really don't belong in that world. I am pleased with what I heard from you. I feel at peace in your presence. Could you tell me a little about your trajectory?

Divine

Of course, yes. I was born in northeastern Brazil, in a family of farmers. Since I was little, I struggled with misery, rejection, and indifference. I grew up in a hostile environment with all kinds of hardship. My childhood dreams were to have toys, food, and books. As I grew up, I had new dreams. I wished to be a writer and filmmaker. But my financial situation was bad, which made things very difficult. I gave up the artistic area several times. After I passed a good public contest, I resumed my dreams. I spent a lot of time writing books and published in some countries around the world. A little later, I became a filmmaker. I am aware that I am on the right path and that I have made great progress. However, being an artist is very complicated by the financial aspect. We don't have any incentive. But I will fight for what I believe as long as I can. Victory belongs to those who believe in their potential.

David

Very cool, your story. You are a warrior. I'm sorry to ask, but I'm curious. Regarding the personal aspect, what is your worldview?

Divine

Currently, I think that love is rare among people. We are in an age of appreciation for material things. Money has become the center of all social relations. However, some enlightened people love and are loved. They are generally evolved spirits who came to teach in this world of atonement and evidences.

David

I agree. These people are so rare that you're the first person I know. So, do you already have your love?

Divine

I haven't found my love yet, but it will appear in my life at some point. I have loved intensely several times. But in all these situations I was not reciprocated. Despite having suffered, I do not regret what I felt. I think it is a path of maturity and evolution. I am proud to have loved someone one day.

David

I understand. Furthermore, I'm in the same situation. No one wants serious relationships nowadays. Nowadays, what predominates is casual sex. I have to follow this trend to have sexual satisfaction. But regardless of anything, I still dream of my prince charming. I wanted to get married and have my children. I wanted to have a happy ending, although the statistics say otherwise.

Divine

I'm rooting for you. Occasionally, I am a conflict of feelings. I've thought about giving up on ever finding love several times. I think of several reasons for staying single. Freedom is my main reason. I am also afraid of my family. I know they wouldn't accept my relationship. So, if I ever find a boyfriend, it has to be a secret.

David

You still have shame about his sexuality. It is understandable. I think you made the right decision. No one needs to know about your happiness, not even your family. Just live happy moments without caring about anything else. I came out as a transsexual. But I am paying a high price.

Divine

I want to avoid paying this price. I will be happy in my own way. Where do you live?

David

In a boring condominium. I have no freedom of speech and I suffer from prejudice. Next month, I am no longer able to pay the rent. I will have to live on the streets.

Divine

This will not happen. Do you want to live with me?

David
Is this serious? I won't be in the way?
Divine
No way. I need company and a friend.
David
I loved it, fag! So, let's rock. Stop the world because the seer and I are going to conquer it.
Divine
So be it, friend.

I am invisible 4

Party
trans
Time to go, faggot! Let's go to the party!
Divine
Cool! This time has finally come. The years of loneliness are over. Finally, I have a friend to keep me company.
Trans
I'm happy to be a part of this special moment. Let's have some fun!
Divine
Yeah, let's go, let's go! Anxiety defines me.
In the bar
Program
James
My name is James. I'm a call-boy. What are your names?
Divine
My name is Divine. But I am also known as "The Seer" or "Son of God".
Transsexual
My name is David. I am a transsexual.
James
What interesting figures. What do you do for a living?

Divine

I'm a civil servant and an artist. But being an artist is just leisure. Truly, my income derives mainly from public service.

David

I am a saleswoman. I sell ice cream and candy on the street.

James

How nice. Elegant and distinct figures. I am a sinner. I live prostituting myself. This is hell, with the forgiveness of the word.

Divine

How do you feel in this world?

James

I feel like an object. Men use me to vent their frustrations. Besides sex, I serve as a psychologist. Usually, they bring problems from home and want to share. Your women don't have time for this. They're very attached to futility.

Divine

Interesting. We all have frustrations. What changes is how each one manages it. Many people get carried away by daily stress and problems. Many end up committing suicide. Others prefer to find ways out and continue to pursue their dreams. They deserve our admiration. We need to continue on with our lives regardless of the issues. We need to react and become protagonists of our history. Only then can we be happy.

James

You said exactly everything. It's a beautiful philosophy. But the world requires more than that. We face difficult practical situations. We are victims of prejudice. Furthermore, we are the scum of society. If it was up to me, I would abandon prostitution. But in a country that doesn't create jobs, that's a viable way out. Besides having pleasure, I help people. That is the positive side of the situation: Collaborate for the well-being of people.

Divine

I get it. Truly, there are these different views of history.

David

I don't understand this demonization of betrayal and sex. We are free people. Marriage is a diabolical invention. End the sexist institution of marriage, and it's only bad for people. The men feel they own their partner and when they want to free themselves, they kill them. It's a perverse domination. Thousands of women lose their lives in that kind of relationship. It's a social massacre where everyone keeps quiet.

Divine

We really are living in genocide. So, I make an appeal to all of us: let's look at relationships and people. You shouldn't trust anyone. It is better to be alone than poorly accompanied.

James

Shall we dance? The time has come.

David

Yeah, let's go, let's go!

Divine

I'm going to sing my song.

Hall

David

We just got here. Did you like the ride?

Divine

I really enjoyed it. It was a great opportunity for reflection.

David

Have you seen our world, Divine? What do you think?

Divine

That it's not the end. Prostitution for many people is a phase. It is a path of learning and evolution. This brings me to a lesson of adolescence: sin is when we hurt others or ourselves. I believe it's a mistake to destroy families and relationships. But perhaps we should think that it is a joint responsibility. The male prostitutes are just doing their job. That's why we shouldn't judge anyone.

David

On that, we agree. We are not to judge each other. That prostitution is not a good way, everyone knows. However, this is necessary for some.

The important thing is reborn at some point in your life. The important thing is to move on and fight. We transsexuals always believe in the happy ending. We are also dreamy human beings. Furthermore, we also have rights and duties as a citizen. So, if you who are "God's child" accepts us, why should I care about the opinions of others? I work and pay my bills. I don't need anyone's approval. Furthermore, I just need a loving friend like you.

Divine

I need you too. The kingdom of God needs it. No more using the Bible to justify atrocities. We need to follow our intuition and know what is right. We need to please God rather than please humanity. May our God be the Holy Spirit instead of money. Only in this way will there be hope for humanity.

David

I do have hope. I'm happy to live with you. You are a talented, intelligent and spiritual person. I really need your strength. It's going to be a great learning period for me.

Divine

That's good, my friend. We learn together and we evolve. Everything will be fine.

David

May God hear you.

I am invisible 5

Trans

I got a surprise for you, buddy! Furthermore, I hope you don't mind.

Divine

What is it this time? May I know? Something serious?

Trans

I invited two friends to come here.

Divine

No problem. Those friends of yours behaved? Do they respect our gender identity?

Trans

I met them on the street. We had a beer together and they seemed really nice.

Divine

It's all right. I believe in your analysis.

Trans

There's only one problem. They said they don't like to invade our privacy. So, we'll wait for them on the terrace.

Divine

All right. Then let's go. I love to watch the stars and talk. I think it will be a good experience.

Trans

I agree. Yes, we will.

Terrace

Bradley

Thank you so much for inviting me, David. It's always good to share interesting moments with people in the same social pond.

David-trans

Thank you very much. We're both very lonely people. We are surrounded on all sides by intolerant, prejudiced and envious people. This is highly stressful. We need people like you.

Robert

I can imagine your situation. We are living in dark times. The world is quite perverse with the LGBT group. We're called freaks and sick people. But we're not like that. We're just human beings with qualities and flaws like anyone else. But this is something of the present. In ancient Greece, homosexuality was seen as something normal as heterosexuality. In fact, prejudice rooted in people was built through the fundamentalism of the dominant Western religions, where we are compared to criminals and excluded from social relations. This fueled hatred through the fanaticism. So, we have come to the conclusion that it is bad for people.

Divine

I agree. I am totally opposed to this false morality. Furthermore, I support and protect minorities. I am the God of the outcast. I sacrificed myself for all of them. These false prophets who live spreading hatred will give an account on the day of judgment. They are like weeds. Nothing produces. The day will come when people will be judged by their works. On that day, there will be weeping and gnashing of teeth.

Bradley

When that time comes, it'll be the end of the world. Well, let me introduce myself to you. My name is Bradley. I'm a romantic guy, demanding, fighting, honest and loyal. Friendship and love are my priorities. But I also enjoy parties, orgies, fishing, bathing in the river, beach and adventure sports.

Divine

I used to like it. My name is Divine and I'm thirty-seven years old. I'm a civil servant and an artist. My main goal is art, but I also love work and travel. I like hanging out with friends, family, co-workers, but I don't go to the parties. I've never been lucky in love. In the professional and loving field, I've been rejected over five hundred times. Despite that, I still believe in my potential. I will never give up my goals. As long as I live, I'll keep fighting. My main characteristics are ethics, honesty, suitability, fidelity, charity and knowing how to listen. I am quite friendly.

Bradley

I like it. It touched me deeply.

Divine

Glad to hear it, young man.

Trans-David

I'm fundamentally different from you. I am more practical. Furthermore, I like casual sex, parties, the media, beach, nature, anyway, I like to enjoy my life in the best way possible. I don't think much about the future because it belongs to God. So, I enjoy the good times life gives me. But I'm also honest and hardworking. I just want what is mine.

Robert

My name is Robert. I look like David. I'm in the same position. Furthermore, I like events, going out, drinking at the bar, sex, having a good time. Moreover, I don't care about the reviews. I'd rather do it than regret it later. I believe that life is a great gift, a great learning. Everyone is moving towards evolution. Some with more capacity and others with less capacity. What makes us the same is being imperfect? So, we can't judge anyone. Just live without caring what people think.

Trans-David

I have a proposition for you. Since we're so much alike. Why aren't we dating?

Robert

Great idea. I date you and Bradley dates Divine. Agreed?

Bradley

I'm going to love. That's a great idea.

Divine

Okay. I'll take that as a joke. How about enjoying life together?

Bradley

If you want it that way, that's fine with me.

Trans-David

Divine loves someone else. But let's pretend we don't know. We're going to have so much fun.

Divine

Regardless, I want to live. Look at the stars and reflect on how special we are. We need to place ourselves in the world with authority. Being the protagonist of your own life is a mission. Let's do it then. Time is of the essence.

Trip to an island- I'm invisible 6

On the shore

Divine

Thank you for being with me. I love the beach. I often stopped coming for lack of company. Your contribution is important to me. I feel at peace.

Bradley

Thank you, my love. I also love being on the beach with friends. I feel complete and happy. Furthermore, I think that's love. Sharing happy moments with no expectation.

Divine

You are absolutely right. Our union brings me good thoughts and pleasure. I feel really happy.

David-trans

This is really cool. It seems we are children of God in this paradise. I feel like anyone else. This is so rare for me. Transsexuality is still very persecuted.

Robert

I don't care about your sexual orientation. I love people. That's why I'm dating you. I'm so happy right now. Nothing else matters. Tomorrow is another day. I don't know what's going to happen. In the future, will remain only memories. Everything in life is fleeting. What remains are the powers of God.

David trans

I'm happy with you, too. Let's make the most of these moments. This beach is a wonderful place. This is where I find my best wishes. I am reborn and believe more in life. I suffer so much with prejudice. You can't imagine the size of the problem. I just wanted to be judged by my works. I just wanted to have the right to work, to attend public places safely and to love freely. Furthermore, I've committed no crime. I am a citizen fulfilling my duties. But they don't respect me. I'm called a freak, an anomaly and a thug. Many times, they even wanted to kill me. It's called gender bias. You homophobic motherfuckers! May God, repay you double what you wish for me. While you're busy hating and stalking, I'm busy doing good deeds. Who is better among us? Society continues to condemn us using the Bible as an argument. But the Bible was written by men thirsting for war and full of prejudice. The God I know is not a God of wars. He is a God of peace, love, and freedom. The prince of peace is called "Jesus Christ". He came to make sense of our lives.

Divine

I don't blame you, either. We have no right to judge anyone. We are all sinners. Furthermore, we came to this planet to evolve. The path of enlightenment is an arduous path that most refuse to follow. They prefer the broad path of doom. It's easier to criticize than act. It's easier to judge than to analyze your mistakes. We are governed by social rules that contribute to a false moral. We're arrested for an invisible dictatorship. However, it should not be so. We are free and owners of our history. We have to defend democracy and freedom at all costs. Furthermore, we need to react and fight for our rights. Progress has already been made, but there is a long way to go. It is up to us to demand a responsible political stance from our rulers. As a representative of the population, the head of state has to govern for everyone. This is not happening in several countries. It's time for a change.

Bradley

Way to go, baby. No more pretending that everything is okay. We need to take our place in the world. Respect and be respected. We need to make a difference for the sake of others and ourselves. Great men are those who fight for social causes. Some of these examples were: Martin Luther King, Nelson Mandela, Teresa of Calcutta, Francis of Assisi and Jesus Christ. Let's follow these good examples and make history. In order to contribute to a better universe, just act. Small gestures also make a difference: an embrace, a council, charity, a word of support, a forgiveness, a fresh start. Being more human must be our priority.

Robert

I must agree with you. This has become worrisome in recent times. I call it compulsive obsession. People wanting to belittle others in the name of power. Competition is caused by savage capitalism. As a consequence, we have materialistic, selfish, ignorant, prejudiced, soulless, and highly destructive people. Human life it becomes banal. Nowadays, people kill for whatever reason. The main victims of these attacks are children, women, homosexuals and transsexuals. We need to change that situation for the better.

Divine

The answer is in God. When the world wanted to be greater than God, it sent a plague that became a worldwide pandemic. Now everyone fears for their own life and is locked inside for fear of a virus. Before, the man had no time for family. All they could think about was work and social commitments. This is an example for us to rethink our values. We need to prioritize what's really important: our happiness. Everything else is fleeting. So, think about it.

I am invisible 7

On the farm- old mill

Old black

Thank you for accepting my invitation. This has been my home since I was born. It is a historical house that was an old sugar plantation in the time of slavery.

Divine

I thank you for this wonderful opportunity. It was a pleasure to meet you. I love to travel and meet new places. I love a beach, contact with nature and people, sun, mountains, enjoy beautiful landscapes among other things. Furthermore, I am an enthusiast. Besides, I have a lot of faith in myself and in the good vibrations of the universe. I believe that everything cooperates for the good.

Bradley

It's good to be here with you, love. It's like an immersion in colonial Brazil. This is part of our rich cultural history. We need to reflect on the past so that we can build new public policies for the future. We will fight to make a country more just and equal. It's the least we can do for our children.

David trans

I feel comfortable here. It seems that gender bias does not reach me here because I am among friends. Connecting with this past is significant to me. It makes me reflect on various aspects of life. Colonial Brazil and slavery were extremely striking in our society. These were dark times, but they also taught us human values. I believe that this system was the beginning of savage capitalism. On one side, plantation owners and political elite, and on the other, black and poor. In the contemporary world, we have entrepreneurs and employees on opposite sides. We continue to copy these models of exploration and prejudice without deep reflection. That is a great danger.

Robert

I agree, baby. We can't refuse to face our problems. That's why we live in society. In a way, we are the forerunners of this new revolution of values and culture. We need to fight for our place in the world. We must create our history with pride. Furthermore, we will not accept submission in the face of recent directives issued by politicians and bosses. We are all children of God and deserve respect.

Black

Okay. I support all of this. I'm also from the LGBT group. Furthermore, I defend our interests with all my courage. We need to establish ourselves as a group and earn rights. The world will still be ours.

Divine

Hopefully. Now tell us a little story about this house.

Black

It will be an honor. Let's start with the historical context. From the 16th century, black Africans were brought to Brazil to work in sugar cane plantations and mining. It is estimated that about four million Africans from different regions arrived in Brazil. The slave regime was a highly strenuous labor regime. Were imposed long hours of hard work, lack of food and adequate sanitary conditions beyond the violence imposed by the bosses. As a consequence, some fled to the countryside in villages called quilombos. An example of this, in our region we had the quilombo called "Serra da Cruz". Well. In this house lived a rich landowner who took advantage of slave labor for a long time. With the abolition of slavery in the nineteenth century, his business failed, and he moved to capital. I am descended from one of the slaves, and now I own this mansion. I feel happy to be part of a twist in the story.

David trans

How Amazing! One team is the hunters, the other is the hunted. Along with black people, we're called minorities in this country. But we have a story to tell and remember. Cruel stories with no happy ending. But not all situations are equal. I think we should to rewrite history. We are solely responsible for our happiness. Always keep that in mind.

Robert

I always say that. Let's forget the criticisms of others and live our lives. Let's think less and act more. Life is so fleeting. So, I enjoy every moment like it's my last. I don't regret any of my decisions, whether they're right or wrong. There is no other way to evolve than to learn from your mistakes.

Bradley

Let's just move on. Let us correct the mistakes of the past and plan for the future. We have everything to work out. We are a vast country, full of natural and human resources. Furthermore, we have a diverse culture, the result of the mixing of peoples. We are the pride of this country. We have a worldwide reputation for being hardworking and dreamy people. Let's not lose that credibility. We are the people who never give up.

Divine

I should know. I am an example of persistence. None of the difficulties I faced made me stop dreaming. Today I have conviction in my projects. Today I believe in happiness and victory because I am worthy of it. In fact, everyone deserves to make any dream come true if you're willing to work hard enough to get it. Faith, courage, determination, and hope are the concepts that will guide me for the rest of my days.

Bradley

It's time to say goodbye. I appreciate the happy times, Divine. But our time is up. It was a pleasure to meet you.

Divine

Thank you. I don't love you, either. Brian will always be my one true love. But our experiences were very fruitful.

Robert

I don't want you either, David. I couldn't bear to assume a transsexual for long. Furthermore, I hope you'll understand and forgive me.

David

Don't worry about it. I thoroughly understand it. I appreciate your contribution in my life. Furthermore, I'll never forget it. Friends for life, huh?

Robert

Of course. You can count on me.

I am invisible- testimony

Divine

We're going to debate transsexuality. What's your story?

Layla

Speech 1

My name is Layla. I am a transsexual. Since childhood, I have not identified me with my biological sex. My attitudes, my tastes, and my toys were all the opposite sex. It caused strangeness and prejudice in my family.

Speech 2

The relationship with my family was getting worse and the only solution was to run away from home. My parents would not accept me, and the person who supported me was my uncle. Thanks to his help, I was able to get financial support so that I could continue studying.

Speech 3

Speaking of school environment, it was a big challenge. No one respected me. I suffered persecution from most of the students. They often attacked me verbally and physically.

Speech 4

Still, I haven't given up studying. The studies were the only chance for life improvement. I had to resist. I needed to become the person I always dreamed of. A person with ethics and values regardless of my sexuality.

Speech 5

When my uncle died, my world collapsed. I dropped out of school, lived on the streets, did drugs and prostituted myself. It was a difficult moment I called "Dark Night of the Soul". I've learned good and evil in these experiments.

Speech 6

That's when I met my mother again. We reconciled and I went back to her place. When I got there, I knew my father had died of a stroke. It hurt me a lot, but I understand it as a sign of fate.

Speech 7

With my mother's support, I resumed my studies and graduated from law school. I continued studying and became a judge. Today I am a public employee and I collaborate with LGBT rights organizations.

Speech 8

I continue to suffer persecution and prejudice because I live in the country that kills most transvestites and transsexuals in the world. But I am a citizen, aware of my rights and duties. I know my value as a human being. I deserve everyone's respect.

Testimony 2- Emily

My name is Emily. I identified myself as a transsexual at the age of thirteen. But I was too scared. I lived in a village where everyone knew about our life. It was very dangerous to assume your sexual identity for society and for the family. I started to plan my life. I came of age and moved to São Paulo. There, I was able to get in touch with an LGBT group. I understood my condition and began my process of sexual transition. I had no money. Therefore, I did this process of knowledge alone, which brought me several consequences. But psychologically, I was better. I felt like a woman. Being transgender, I suffer a lot of aggression from homophobic groups. But I remain alive and with hope. I live in the most prejudiced country in the world, and this is a great challenge. I think society should reevaluate its values. Why are we compared to bandits? I am a citizen fulfilling my duties and this should be respected. All minorities suffer in this country and this has to be denounced to the world. We have a right to our choices. We deserve to live. I will continue to fight for my rights tirelessly.

Testimony 3- Daisy

You can call me Daisy. I'm from Rio de Janeiro. Born into the upper class, in a so-called conservative family, I remained in the closet until I was twenty when I moved. The change of residence brought a new dynamic to my life. I started my sexual transition and I took advantage of my freedom. At every event, I was participating. They were crazy situations where I tasted everything: orgy, drugs, group trips and parties. They were overwhelming periods of happiness, but they left me with sequels. I was infected with HIV and became chemically dependent. It was ten years of prostration. Until I met a boy, an engineer. He became my companion and was very supportive. We lived together for ten years, and it was enough for me to get rid of all the vices. We split up later, but we stayed friends. My experience has shown me that love liberates. That's what the world needs: love, understanding and tolerance.

Divine

What should I say? You're all special to me. I admire your courage and ask God to bless you. You are marking history in this country so that in the future, transsexuals will be respected. I believe the world will evolve. Congratulations to you all.

The End

www.ingramcontent.com/pod-product-compliance
Lightning Source LLC
LaVergne TN
LVHW020454080526
838202LV00055B/5441